SHAKE IT OFF!

VANESSA BRANTLEY-NEWTON

Nancy Paulsen Books

For every child who has been counted out . . .
You weren't meant to blend in, but to stand out.
Shake it off and stand out.

NANCY PAULSEN BOOKS
An imprint of Penguin Random House LLC, New York

First published in the United States of America by Nancy Paulsen Books,
an imprint of Penguin Random House LLC, 2024

Visit us online at PenguinRandomHouse.com.

Library of Congress Cataloging-in-Publication Data
Names: Brantley-Newton, Vanessa, author, illustrator.
Title: Shake it off / Vanessa Brantley-Newton.
Description: New York: Nancy Paulsen Books, 2024. | Summary: After getting stuck in a well,
a clever little goat finds a way to rescue herself.
Identifiers: LCCN 2023017252 | ISBN 9780525517115 (hardcover) | ISBN 9780525517122 (ebook) |
ISBN 9780525517139 (kindle edition)
Subjects: CYAC: Goats—Fiction. | Problem solving—Fiction. | Self-reliance—Fiction. |
LCGFT: Animal fiction. | Picture books.
Classification: LCC PZ7.1.B75153 Sh 2024 | DDC [E]—dc23
LC record available at https://lccn.loc.gov/2023017252

Manufactured in China
ISBN 9780525517115
1 3 5 7 9 10 8 6 4 2
TOPL

Edited by Nancy Paulsen | Art direction by Cecilia Yung
Design by Eileen Savage | Text set in Palatino Sans
The artwork was hand drawn and then colored using Adobe Photoshop and Corel Painter.

This *is* a story that will have
a happy ending, so don't
worry too much!

There once was a little goat.

The little goat loved to sing. In the morning you could always hear her!

BAAAA, BAAAA, BAAAA . . .

She loved to climb—on rocks, trees, and roofs!

The neighbors thought the goat
was *so* annoying!

One day, the farmers had to go to town.
The little goat decided she should go on
an adventure too.

As she started walking, she accidentally fell down into an old well.

Oh no! This was not the kind of adventure the *little* goat was *looking for!*

Her cries were so loud that the neighbors came running.

They were surprised to find the goat stuck at the bottom of the deep well.

Oh my goodness!

The little goat was a good climber, but even she could not climb out of this.

The neighbors discussed how to rescue her.

"Let's get a ladder!"

"It's not big enough."

"How about a rope?"

"It's not long enough."

Then someone said, "Well, getting her out is impossible, so we might as well give her a decent burial. It's sad, but she was pretty annoying."

So they got their shovels and began
to throw dirt into the well.

Of course, when the little
goat felt the dirt on her back,
she did not like it at all!
So she shook that dirt right
off and packed it under.

With every shovelful of dirt, the
little goat would sing to herself:

"Shake it off. Pack it under!
Shake it off. Pack it under!"

And then something
wonderful happened.
The goat rose out of the
well on the heap of dirt that
had been meant to bury her!

The neighbors could not
believe it. "What an amazing goat,"
they said as they headed home.

When the farmers returned, they
were surprised the goat was so dirty.

"What on earth happened?"
they asked.

The little goat just bleated softly
and shook herself from nose to tail.

"Shake it off!"

From then on, whenever the neighbors heard the goat, they smiled and said, "Such a remarkable little goat!"

Ahhh, a happy ending!

Author's Note

As a little girl, I was often afraid to speak because I stuttered, and it also took me a while to read because I have something called dyslexia. In school I got picked on, and when I would share my pain with my mother, she'd encourage me to shake off other people's opinions and judgments about me. It wasn't easy to do that at first, but the more I did it, the easier it got, and I began to believe in myself. I found that shaking off the negativity we encounter is a vital step toward living our best lives. I also discovered that I could use my experiences as stepping stones to rise above the negativity and strengthen my resilience so I could face future challenges with courage, determination, and a sense of humor. Remember, it's not about ignoring these experiences, but rather learning from them. I hope that reading *Shake It Off!* will help empower you to live your best life and be proud in front of the world. When you learn to shake it off, you can then climb the highest peaks!